SMILE IF YOU'RE HUMAN

ISBN 0-439-18690-0

Published by Scholastic Inc., 555 Broadway, New York, NY 10012,
by arrangement with Dial Books for Young Readers, a member of Penguin Putnam Inc.

12 11 10 9 8 7 6 5 4 3 2 1 0 1 2 3 4 5/0

Printed in the U.S.A. 08

First Scholastic printing, April 2000

Published in Great Britain in 1998 by Bloomsbury Publishing Plc. as *The Photo*
Typography by Debora Smith

SMILE IF YOU'RE HUMAN

story and pictures by *Neal Layton*

SCHOLASTIC INC.
New York Toronto London Auckland Sydney
Mexico City New Delhi Hong Kong

HERE we are landing at a place
I've wanted to visit my whole life.
It's a planet called "Earth."

On Planet Earth there are
many animals.

I've brought my camera and hope to take a picture of a most unusual creature known as a "human."

We thought we saw one hopping around
in a green circular thing. "Is that a human?"
I asked my mom.

Mom looked at her book. "This jumpy fellow is a kangaroo. Humans like to walk."

As we spotted another animal,
I got my camera ready. "Look, Dad!
Humans are covered with stripes!"

"Hmm," said Dad, "I don't think so. They don't have tails and they mostly stand on two feet."

I raced up ahead.

"What about these? They walk on two feet, and they seem very smart. They must be humans.

"They are smart," said Dad,
"but they're penguins.

Humans don't have wings or webbed feet."

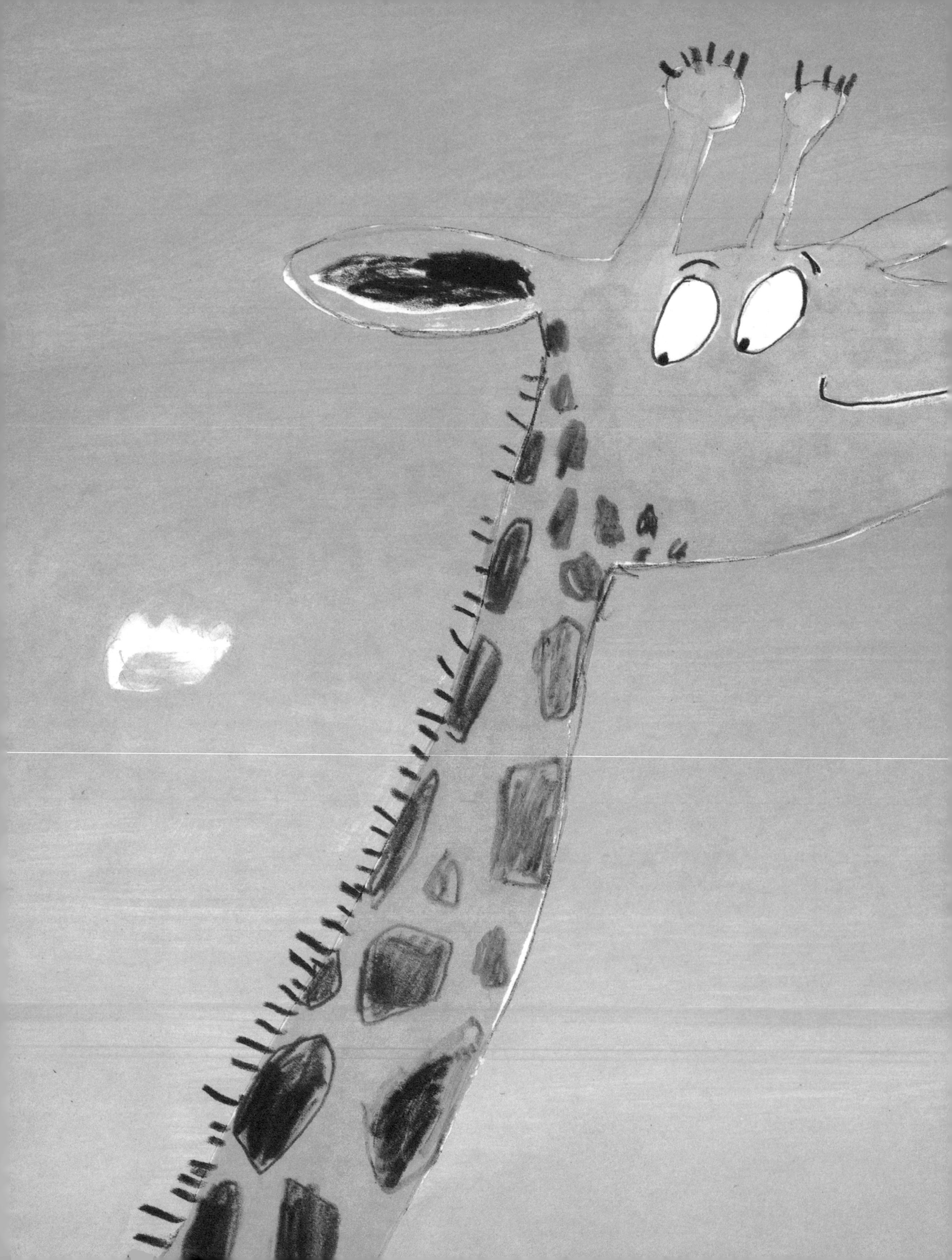

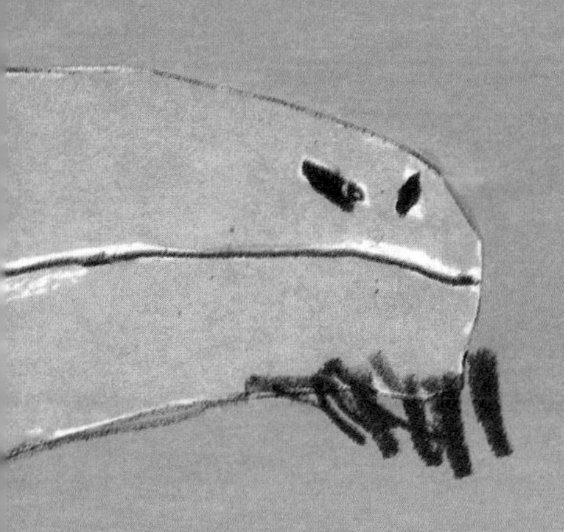

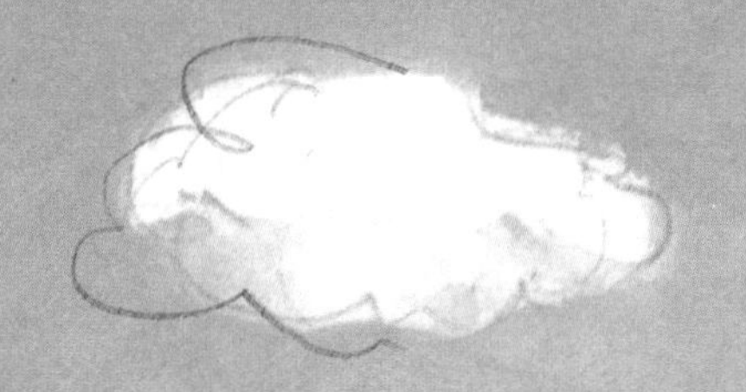

Just then I looked way, way up and was sure I'd discovered a human. "Wow, they're really tall!"

"Some humans are tall," Mom explained, "but not **that** tall. This is a giraffe."

We had looked around
nearly the whole planet.

In the last house, we saw a
mysterious creature peeking out.

We got closer and I could see that it was . . .
the most stupendous animal ever!

"Is it? IS IT?

"YES, IT IS!"

"IT COULD DO WITH A HAIRCUT, THOUGH!"

ALIENS'
GUIDE
TO
EARTH

I steadied my camera,
took careful aim, and

CLICK!

And here it is—

They don't have tails, or wings, or webbed feet; they're not great hoppers, or all **that** tall. But one thing for sure about humans—***they have the greatest smiles!***